ONE OF TH

WESLEY'S ESS

THE GHOSTS OF BORLEY

LEGENDS, GHOSTS, HAUNTINGS, INTRIGUES

and

UNSOLVED MYSTERIES

Plus

STORIES OF GHOSTS AND HAUNTINGS

ALONG THE

ESSEX AND SUFFOLK BORDER

WESLEY H. DOWNES

£3.95

ISBN 0 9519289 4 5

Published by Wesley's Publications, 61 Lymington Avenue, Clacton-on-Sea, Essex CO15 4QE.

First Published 1993.

Front Cover and Drawings by Rose Bishop.
Printed and Typeset by
Guild Press (Clacton), Clacton-on-Sea, Essex.

AUTHOR'S ACKNOWLEDGEMENTS

I am greatly indebted to all who have contributed stories and information so freely to me, and duly acknowledge the authors of previously published works.

To Paul Kemp, who allowed me access to many years of his Borley investigations and researches.

Also to Geoff and Anthea Holland for the use of their photographs.

A special word of thanks to my good friend George, for the hours he spent reading and correcting the manuscript, also to my wife for her patience in looking at my back for hours on end while I work at my word processor - Patience is a virtue.

Lastly, but not least, to Rose Bishop for the high quality of her drawings, also to Colin, Janet and all the staff at Guild Press for the high standard of their work.

Thank you all.

INTRODUCTION

'Borley', became famous in June 1929, when the Rector, the Rev. G. E. Smith, wrote to the Daily Mirror asking them to investigate the mysterious happenings at Borley Rectory.

Since then, the name Borley has been synonymous with ghosts and hauntings, thanks to the late Harry Price, a psychic investigator, who was asked to carry out the investigation.

In 1937, Price rented the then empty Rectory for a year, with the view to study, record and confirm some of the previously reported 'happenings'.

After placing an advertisement in The Times, he enlisted the assistance of dozens of investigators to spend time in the house to keep a record of any phenomena that might occur.

In 1940, Price created considerable interest when he published his book 'The Most Haunted House in England', followed in 1946, by 'The End of Borley Rectory'.

Both these books reveal some of the history of Borley Rectory and accounts of its hauntings and other forms of phenomena, plus the experiences of those who spent their days and nights during that year of investigation.

The Rectory was mysteriously destroyed by fire on the night of February 27th 1939, but since then, there have been hundreds of reported sightings of ghosts on or near the site despite the fact that nothing remains of the Rectory, just a neat row of bungalows and a path called The Nuns Walk!

Although Borley found fame because of the reported haunting of the Rectory, one could almost say that Borley Church was, and still is, equally well known for its own 'unexplained happenings'.

Nearby Borley Place, can also stake a claim in the history of hauntings. Yes indeed, Borley most certainly rates high in league for the 'Most Haunted Village in England'!!

Just in case the reader should become bored with reading about Borley, (sorry about the pun) there are a number of other stories of hauntings along the Essex/Suffolk border which I hope that you will also enjoy reading.

W.H.D.

CONTENTS

THE BACKGROUND TO BORLEY RECTORY

If ever a house was built to be haunted, then it must surely have been Borley Rectory.

It was built in 1863 on the site of an earlier Rectory which was burned down in 1841, and that in turn had allegedly been built partly on the site of an old monastery.

The 1863 Rectory was built by the Reverend Henry Dawson Ellis Bull, the Rector of Borley and it was an ugly building to start with. It had high gabled walls with a strange looking tower over the front door and its appearance was certainly not improved by many necessary additions as the size of Rev Henry Bull's family increased.

Henry Bull eventually had fourteen children, therefore it is easy to understand why in 1875, apart from previous additions, he was obliged to add a completely new wing.

To put things in their correct sequence, a potted history of Borley might help the reader appreciate the situation.

In 1362, King Edward III granted the manor of Borley to the Order of the Benedictine Monks who duly built a monastery. However, the manor somehow remained in the Waldegrave family for the next three hundred years and for much of that time they supported the monks.

In due course, the monastery ceased to be used and was eventually demolished. Whether or not this was due to King Henry VIII and the Dissolution of the Monasteries Act of 1538, is uncertain.

It was usual in the 18th and 19th centuries, for the Lords of the Manor to appoint and support the clergy to the churches within their manor. Therefore, it was no great surprise when, in 1862, a relative of the Waldegraves, Rev H. D. E. Bull became the Rector of Borley.

He wasted no time in making plans to build his Rectory on the site of the old monastery which was conveniently opposite the church.

Rev Henry Bull came from a family of clerics and his father, Rev Edward Bull was rector of nearby Pentlow. The clerical Bull's seemed to stem from about 1752.

When Henry died in 1892 in Borley Rectory, he was succeeded by his son, Rev Henry Foyster Bull, who was generally known as 'Harry' Bull to avoid any confusion between father and son.

Harry Bull lived in the Rectory until he died in 1927. After his death the Rectory stood empty for some time until the Rev Guy Eric Smith took over the living in October 1928.

It was not long after the Smith's arrived at Borley that the Rev Smith appealed to the Daily Mirror newspaper for help to investigate the 'strange occurrences' there.

In February 1939 the Rectory was virtually destroyed by fire and later the remains were demolished and later still a neat row of bungalows were erected on the site.

During the demolition and site clearing in 1943 of the Rectory remains, a human skull was found in one of the cellars. Apart from the fact it was female and very old, nothing else was established about it.

Of course, this led to rumours of it belonging to the legendary nun, or to one of the maids, who rumour had it, disappeared many years before and was believed to have been murdered there. However, the skull was later interred in nearby Liston churchyard.

****

A report in the Suffolk & Essex Free Press dated Thursday, June 13th. 1929, states that a London domestic who, two days after entering the Rectory and knowing nothing of the past history, almost went off in a dead faint as she informed her mistress that she had seen a nun dressed in black.

EARLY REPORTED SIGHTINGS

Some of the earliest recorded sightings of ghosts at Borley Rectory were by four of Rev Henry Bull's daughters. On the afternoon of July 28th 1900, three of the girls were approaching the rectory gate from the lane, when all three clearly saw a figure they all thought was that of a nun gliding along the path that within living memory had never been known other than as 'Nun's Walk'.

Although the figure appeared to be as solid as that of a normal human being, none of them actually saw her face.

One of the girls ran into the house to get the other sister to come and see the 'ghost'. When she arrived, the figure was still in sight, but she did not believe it was an apparition and immediately approached with the intention of asking the nun who she was looking for, but just before she reached the figure, it vanished.

Another early report of the figure of a nun being seen within in the grounds of the rectory, was related by a former headmaster of Colchester Royal Grammar School, who frequently visited Borley Rectory. He stated that he had seen the 'nun' several times during his visits in 1885/6 and when he discussed the matter with the Rev Harry Bull, he too, declared that he had seen the ghostly nun several times, both before and after his father died.

Legend has it, that many years ago, long before the rectory was built, a novice nun from the nunnery at nearby Bures, fell in love with one of the lay brothers from Borley monastery. Their meeting place was in a secluded glade in the middle of the woods close to Borley.

There has always been a legend of a tunnel connecting the nunnery at Bures and the monastery at Borley with a possible branch leading to Borley Church; also there have been rumours of there being several exits along the seven mile length of the tunnel, many of them actually in the woods. Therefore it might have been possible for the 'lovers' to have made use of a part of the tunnel system for their meetings.

However, the story unfolds to the time when they decided to leave their respective Orders and elope.

The monk confided their plan to an acquaintance who was able to arrange for a carriage to pick them both up at a given time and place.

All went well so far, the night chosen happened to be a brilliant moonlit night, the carriage arrived at the appointed time and place and the lovers climbed aboard and off they went.

Unfortunately, they were both missed from their quarters and a party was sent on horseback to find them. The carriage had only travelled a few miles before it was stopped and the couple removed.

In those days, to run away from religious Orders was a very serious offence and the punishment was invariably - death.

Legend has it that the lay brother was hung and the novice nun was bricked up alive in a niche in the nunnery wall with just the traditional loaf of bread and a pitcher of water.

It was not long before stories circulated that the villagers of Borley had seen a spectral nun walking along near - and sometimes within - the grounds of the monastery with her hands clasped together in front of her as if she were praying.

Not only were there tales of the ghostly nun, but also of a phantom coach and horses coming along the lane and swinging into the driveway of the Rectory, following the circular route of the old drive and ending up near the front of the old rectory and then vanishing.

Many people over the years claim to have witnessed this phenomena, some say they have seen the figure of the nun inside the carriage, others that both the nun and the driver (sometimes two drivers) have been headless, some even say that the horses appeared to be headless as well.

A local policeman recalled he was on cycle patrol late one night and on his way to make a 'point' with another constable from the next village. As it was a warm, bright moonlit evening, he was pushing his cycle up the slight hill just past the site of the Rectory, when he heard the sound of horses hooves and the iron clad wheels coming towards him.

He immediately pulled his cycle close to the side of the road and stood and waited for the vehicle to pass. The sound came closer and he felt a breeze as it passed, but there was nothing to be seen. He was the good old-time fearless type of policeman, but he admitted that the experience did un-nerve him and he was glad when his duty was complete that night.

One evening in March 1939, a gardener who, despite the fire, still worked at the Rectory, was cycling home to Borley Green, when he heard the sound of horses trotting down the hill. He dismounted and pulled his cycle on to the grass at the side of the road, at the same time turning his lamp in the direction of the sounds. To his amazement, the sounds of trotting horses passed right by him and on down the hill, but there was nothing to be seen.

This same gardener had also seen mysterious lights in the rectory windows both before and after the fire.

****

Mrs Smith, the wife of Rev Smith, even took some villagers into the Rectory after these same mysterious lights had been pointed out to her, but on entering the affected bedroom there was no sign of any light, yet back outside it was still shining brightly. Several other villagers have seen these illuminated windows many times.

THE BULL DYNASTY

When Rev Henry Bull built his rectory, little did he know just what a 'can of worms' he was opening.

He was something of an eccentric, wearing his clerical dress only on Sundays and he relaxed by lying on the drawing-room floor with the casement window open, taking pot shots with a rifle at rabbits on the lawn. He was also a keen horseman and often rode with the local hounds.

Apart from his daughters' seeing the ghost of the nun, one of them said she woke to see the figure of an old man in dark, old-fashioned clothes, wearing a tall hat, standing by her bed.

When he died in 1892, it was in the Rectory's 'Blue Room' and it was this room on the first floor where there were many manifestations. Rev Henry Bull had several times mentioned that he had witnessed them, but this still did not stop him from sleeping there.

He was followed by his son, Rev 'Harry' Bull, also an eccentric and one of his odd habits was to wander into the rectory grounds and fall asleep for hours on end. It was said that he kept about thirty cats who would follow him everywhere.

Having been brought up to live with the legend of the ghostly nun, one of the first things he did when he took over the living, was to build a summer house on the lawn so that he could sit and watch for her taking her frequent walks. He had quite an interest and belief in the supernatural and was said to have warned his family that he would let them know that he was still keeping an eye on them from beyond the grave by throwing mothballs. In actual fact, mothballs were later thrown about!!

However, he did not marry until he was forty-eight years of age, and then it was to a twenty-nine year old widowed shopkeeper from nearby Sudbury. This marriage certainly did not meet with the approval of his spinster sisters, who could see themselves not only losing out on the family finances, but also she would become the mistress of the house and could 'lord it' over them.

The marriage lasted for sixteen years until 1927 when Harry died in the 'Blue Room', allegedly from chronic bronchitis, although there were strong rumours circulating that he may have been poisoned by his wife. It does not take much imagination to realise that these rumours were probably spread by his sisters to show their hatred of their sister-in-law.

Because of Harry's threat to return to haunt the Rectory, everybody waited to see if he was able to keep his word, which he obviously did, for not only were mothballs thrown about from time to time, but his ghostly figure has also been seen and identified.

ENTER THE SMITH'S AND FOYSTER'S

After Harry's death, the Rectory remained empty until 1928 when the Rev Guy Eric Smith, an Anglo-Indian and his English wife arrived to take up the vacant living.

Although the use of the Rectory automatically went with the living, the Smith's preferred to live mainly in Long Melford. Whether or not their choice of living away from Borley was influenced by tales of the hauntings or the size and condition of the Rectory is not known.

However, one thing is certain, Rev Smith was sufficiently concerned about the hauntings to write to the Daily Mirror newspaper asking for help.

One day Mrs Smith found among other things a paper wrapped parcel. It contained the skull of a young woman in perfect condition as were the teeth. Rev Smith and the Sexton buried it in the churchyard.

One summer afternoon in 1928, when Rev Smith was alone in the house, he left his bedroom and was coming through an archway on the landing when he distinctly heard whispering over his head. The sounds followed him until he reached the archway leading to the chapel when the whispering stopped abruptly.

Subsequently he heard the same sounds many times along this landing, but one day he was startled in the same area by a moaning sound gradually rising in tone and ended with the words "Don't Carlos, don't". Sometime later he found out that 'Carlos' was the family nick-name for Henry Bull.

After about eighteen months, the Smiths' gave up the living and moved away altogether.

The next occupier of the Rectory was Rev Lionel Algernon Foyster, a relative of the Bull's. His wife Marianne was much younger by some twenty years and although they had no children of their own, they did have an adopted girl aged between two and three years, named Adelaide.

It was about this time that the manifestations were most active, sufficiently so, for Rev Foyster to keep a diary of what he regarded as 'supernatural events'.

In due course the Foyster's too, moved out, or perhaps to be more precise, were driven out.

However, by this time, the psychic investigator Harry Price was deeply involved with the case and he took the opportunity to rent the Rectory for a year so that he could, with the aid of enlisted helpers, carry out continuous investigations.

A SUMMARY OF HARRY PRICE'S INVESTIGATIONS

Throughout the year Harry Price rented the Rectory, many investigators took part and subsequently reported their experiences both outside and inside the building.

In many instances, various phenomenon was witnessed by as many as four people at a time, ranging from the ringing of door and servants call bells, despite the fact that the wires had been disconnected because of their continual ringing, a candlestick taken from a bedroom and thrown down the stairs, flying stones, slates thrown from the roof, bottles manifesting and flying through the air, hot coals appearing from nowhere and starting small fires.

Several times footsteps were heard walking across bedroom floors, along passages and up and down the stairs, but there was never any sign of who or what was making them.

Mysterious writing appeared on walls, the name 'Marianne' was written several times, remember, that was the name of Rev Foyster's wife and by this time, the Foyster's had moved out. Other words also appeared and when questions were written by the investigators, answers would sometimes appear.

Strange rapping's, whispering and voices were often heard when the investigators on duty were together either resting or reading, so it certainly was not due to them talking amongst themselves.

Many times from the outside of the building, lights were observed showing from windows, but not always the same window.

Strangely, despite there being well over a hundred different types of manifestations, only a few times were there reports of actual sightings of figures and when there were, it was confined to apparitions of Rev Harry Bull and the mysterious nun.

At a psychic meeting in London on the 27th March 1938, a planchette board was used and an entity prophesied that the rectory would be destroyed by fire. This prophesy did in fact come true on February 27th 1939 and the ruin was finally demolished in 1944.

RECTORY UPDATE 1970 - 80

Even after all signs of the Rectory had been cleared away and the site levelled, reports of sightings of the ghostly nun and the phantom carriage were still made, not only by the dozens of amateur 'psychic investigators' who tend to make life for the local inhabitants unbearable, but also by completely disinterested people who just happen to be passing at the 'wrong' time.

Despite the fact that several writers have set out to destroy Harry Price's findings, there are quite a number who do believe that most of the phenomenon claimed to have been witnessed, really did happen.

Today, over fifty years after the fire, there are still reports of frequent sightings. Organised groups of dedicated investigators still spend night after night with the latest sophisticated equipment, recording every movement and temperature change.

One such group made the following report of their experiences over a ten year period from 1970 to 1980.

During this period they recorded numerous unexplained sounds on tape and also a confirmed sighting of a spectral nun on the site of the Rectory.

To have a sighting 'confirmed', it has to be actually seen by two or more people at the same time.

The confirmed sighting of the nun took place at 1.45 a.m. on the 20th June 1970. One member of the team was patrolling along Nun's Walk behind the new bungalows next to the site of the old Rectory when, in the bright moonlight, he saw the figure of a nun coming towards him along the path. He stood back against the fence and remained still, but watching the figure all the time.

The nun continued towards him, then turned into a hedge, and at this point he used his 'walkie talkie' to contact another member of the team to come slowly towards him.

Just as his colleague came into his view, the nun reappeared through the hedge and continued towards him, so that the nun was actually between the two men and being bright moonlight, they both had a good view of her at the same time.

She then glided away to the back of a bungalow, through the garage, then came back again passing within six feet of the two men. She stopped and stood still for some 30 seconds, then carried on. They had a perfect close up view of her face which appeared to show a great deal of sadness, but what amazed them both was the face was that of an older woman with a mole on her left cheek. All previous reports of sightings have referred to the nun as being young!!

However, the figure completely ignored the two watchers and passed through the hedge again, but this time she appeared to glide about a foot above the ground and to be following an old path until she reached a large heap of brick rubble at the bottom of the garden where she seemed to disappear into the heap, but did not re-appear on the other side.

She was visible for about 9 - 11 minutes, about seven of which she was in view of both men.

On another occasion, two members of the same team were standing outside one of the bungalows that have now been built on the site of the Rectory. It was about 2.30 a.m. when they both heard the slow tread of footsteps coming from about the centre of the garden, on to the road and up the hill towards Rectory Cottage. They estimated that the sounds lasted for about 15 - 20 seconds.

About a year later, on a clear moonlight night, two members of that same group were patrolling along Nun's Walk behind the bungalows when they heard a rustling in the long grass the other side of the fence; they were amazed to see the grass parting as if some large animal were approaching through it - but there was nothing to be seen, then there was a crash against the fence which rattled and a thumping on the ground was both heard and felt, but still nothing was visible.

A few minutes later the branches of a fruit tree started to bend and rustle just as if there were a high wind blowing, but in fact there was no wind at all, there was just nothing to be seen or to account for the movement!!

Researching into some of the claims of various people to have seen the ghostly nun, it would appear that she nearly always takes the same route, although the time of day or night varies. She seems to manifest at the far end of Nun's Walk as it is today, then glide along a path that used to pass through the old Rectory garden, usually stopping to look through what used to be a window in the Rectory, then heading for the church using the path behind the new bungalows.

Although the nun appears to stop and look through where a window used to be in the Rectory, it must not be forgotten that a part of the Rectory was built on the site of a previous monastery - could she have been looking through a monastery window??

In the 1970's, the late Dr Peter Hilton-Rowe, an ex-Bank of England official, was showing an American friend where the Rectory used to stand, when they both saw the figure of a nun gliding along Nun's Walk to eventually disappear in the churchyard.

****

In the period between the fire and the demolition of the Rectory, many people reported that when they were standing at the Rectory gate, 'a great black cat' forces its way between their legs like a bullet and heads for the house like a shot out of a gun, but has never been seen to come out again.

****

It has been said that whilst the fire was raging at the Rectory, many of the onlookers claimed to have seen the face of a woman moving from window to window as if looking for a way of escape and there was much speculation that this was the phantom nun, as no human could have lived in such an inferno.

Others claimed to have seen the figure of a young woman hanging by her finger tips from the window sill of the 'blue room' during the fire.

****

At 10.45 p.m. on 31st May 1978, some members of a research society saw a luminous grey figure in the Rectory orchard. It appeared to be about four feet high, two feet wide and appeared to be hovering about two to two feet six inches above the ground. The shape was visible for about 8-10 seconds.

It moved to the spot where the stables used to be and carriages were kept - could it have come to see the horses?

Although it was not possible to be positive, it was thought to be the apparition of a nun. Research shows that the shape was actually following the known path that the nuns often took when going from the old monastery to buildings where the horses were stabled and the carriages were kept.

Several local people have confirmed seeing the same thing along this same path.

STRANGE HAPPENINGS AT A DINNER PARTY

A very unusual story has been told of the occasion when the Rev and Mrs Foyster were in occupation of Borley Rectory and Mrs Foyster was entertaining a friend to dinner.

Mrs Foyster and her guest were sitting chatting at the dining table waiting for the maid to bring in the food. As the maid came through the doorway with a tray in her hands, a wine bottle suddenly manifested in mid air, and flew across the room to smash under Mrs Foysters chair.

No sooner had they recovered from the shock, when a second bottle appeared and repeated the performance, but this time, smashing under the guest's chair .

By this time Mrs Foyster, her guest and the maid were standing horrified at this sudden outburst; then, a third bottle suddenly flew across the room and stopped in mid air directly in front of them, changed shape into the form of a large mushroom, back to the shape of a normal bottle and then shattered in mid air.

This was just a typical example of the phenomena that occurred at Borley from time to time.

****

A SHOCK FOR THE VISITORS

In the late 1930's, while visiting some friends in Borley, a gentleman and his wife decided to visit the Rectory.

Finding the house empty and the front door swinging open, they decided to look inside. On entering the hall they made their way into what they now know was the Study. Hanging on a wall there was a very large three piece mirror. They stood looking into it, and they both saw the reflection of a middle aged nun, dressed in a very old fashioned heavy cowled type habit with a white wimple, standing behind them.

Turning round, fully prepared to apologise for being inside the house, they were both amazed to find that they were alone in the room!!

It goes without saying, they soon left the Rectory without exploring any further.

BORLEY CHURCH

THE WALDEGRAVE MYSTERIES

Although Borley's reputation was made famous by the Rectory, many people will agree that the church can rightly claim to have as much, if not more mystery, intrigue and hauntings associated with it.

Inside the church there is a monument in the form of an altar tomb to the Waldegrave family. It stands some fourteen feet in height, with six Corinthian columns supporting a canopy. There are two recumbent effigies of Sir Edward Waldegrave and his wife Frances in sixteenth century dress and around the sides are the kneeling figures of their three sons and three daughters.

The Waldegraves were a very important and influential family both locally and nationally. Sir Edward was knighted in 1553, at the coronation of Queen Mary I.

At the time of the Reformation, Sir Edward held a high position in the household of Princess Mary, who was imprisoned for her religious beliefs. Although having been given orders to forbid mass to be said, being a papist himself, he gave in to the Princess and was himself imprisoned in the Tower of London.

When Mary eventually came to the throne, he was released and all his powers restored. Five years later, Queen Elizabeth came to the throne and once again he was sent to the Tower, where he remained until his death on September 1st 1561.

His body was taken back to Borley for burial in a church that had already adopted the revised prayer book of the reformed Church and this is what a small section of people believe he cannot accept and the disturbances within the church are his way of showing his disapproval.

There is also a mystery regarding the Waldegrave vault. So far nobody has found a way to get into it, several stone-masons have examined it, but all have come away scratching their heads, and offering no suggestions!

In 1943, a large flat slab which lay beneath the chancel steps and was always believed to have been the entrance to the Waldegrave vault, was raised, but it turned out to be the original stone altar, which was later restored to its original position.

THE MYSTERY OF THE CHURCH VALUABLES

There is another mystery, this time concerning some missing church plate and valuables. Legend has it, that at the time when Oliver Cromwell's men were plundering the churches, the wise clergy of Borley decided to bury most of the plate etc. in the churchyard until better times. But the trouble was, with everything being carried out with great secrecy, nobody made a note of where it was eventually buried in case the record should be discovered and the position given away. With the passage of time, the location was forgotten and to this day has not been found.

Some years ago a diviner tried to locate this treasure, but failed to do so, but found what was believed to have been a tunnel running from the church, under the road, towards the site of the old Rectory.

****

A lady diviner who was experienced at divining for metals offered to try her skill at locating the legendary buried church valuables with a hazel twig.

One morning she arrived with three men from the B.B.C. to assist her, no doubt they were hoping for a good story should anything be found.

After failing to locate anything in the churchyard, they moved to an adjoining garden. Almost immediately the hazel twig twisted and turned almost uncontrollably near a large walnut tree. Convinced that there was a large metallic object of some sort buried at this spot, the men started digging. Nearly two hours later and with a hole some nine feet deep, the men called a halt to the digging, despite the fact that the hazel twig still twisted and turned over the hole. With time slipping by, and the clouds threatening rain at any minute, they reluctantly decided to back fill the hole and call it a day.

No sooner had they filled the hole than the wind rose and heavy rain fell. That night an almighty storm hit the area. In nearby Foxearth the church steeple was blown down and in Borley, the huge Walnut tree was uprooted and fell right across the very spot where they had been digging.

Taking that as an omen, no further excavating was carried out and the missing valuables still have not been found.

WHO MOVES THE COFFINS?

Many times over the years, heavy stone coffins in the crypt of this old twelfth century church, have been moved from their allocated places and left poised at odd angles.

Each time when, with great difficulty, the coffins have been restored to their correct places, but when next inspected, despite the entrance having been sealed, they are found scattered again, the seals still being intact.

This 'vandalism' could have only have been carried out by some supernatural force.

In 1987/8, a group of local investigators set out to find what they believed was an entrance to the crypt from the churchyard. After spending several unsuccessful hours searching, one of the group discovered a vault with no epitaph that was surrounded by iron railings. One of the team climbed over the ironwork and tapped some of the paving slabs, one in particular sounded hollow, so he gently lifted it to reveal some broken brick steps leading to a tunnel; slowly entering, he was able to walk some thirty feet when he encountered a skeleton near a metal staved wooden door.

Shining a torch through the keynote, he was able to see a small altar and a coffin, a large bundle of papers on the floor and a passageway with a door bearing a plaque inscribed Anno Domini 1921 H.F.B. Obviously Henry Foyster Bull.

The crypt entrance was found to be directly under the present altar inside the church.

GHOSTS IN AND AROUND THE CHURCH

With all the alleged haunting across the road at the Rectory, surely it would be unreasonable to expect there to be even more at the church, but this is where one would be wrong.

The legendary nun has been seen several times in the churchyard, also the ghost believed to be that of a teenaged girl dressed in blue. Some people have also claimed to have seen a veiled woman near to the church, whether she and the nun are one and the same it is difficult to be sure.

Inside the church itself, there are areas which have the reputation of suddenly becoming 'cold' and with a feeling of 'tension' around them. There is a story of a young boy who, with his parents, was visiting the church. As they were walking up the aisle, the boy suddenly stood rigidly still as if frozen to the spot, stared straight ahead wide eyed and after what seemed an age, he burst into tears and ran from the church. His parents tried to get him to explain what had happened, but all he would say was "so cold".

There have been reports of people hearing the organ being played when there has been no organist present and at other times when the church has been locked. Odd sounds have often been heard within and reports of ghostly figures having been seen for split seconds.

In 1980, two psychic investigators were sitting quietly in the church, when suddenly they both saw the figure of a tall man dressed in black old-fashioned clothes manifest and slowly walk along the aisle. They decided to try to find out who he might have been. After months of research they came to the conclusion that he was John Deeks, the vicar at the time of Cromwell.

The same researchers believe that the two nuns often seen in the vicinity of the church could well be Arabella Waldegrave and her mother Henrietta. Henrietta died in 1730 whilst working as a spy for the then Government and was buried at Langenhoe. Arabella was murdered in 1697 spying for the Stuarts, the opposite side to her mother. The whereabouts of her grave is not known, but it seems that their spirits are now re-united and have returned to the family church.

****

CHURCH BELLS

The ringing of church bells at a funeral was thought to scare away the dead person's ghost.

THE BLANK FILM

In 1956 a gentleman staying at Sudbury decided to make a visit to Borley Church with a friend.

After walking around the churchyard and taking photographs of a number of old tombstones, they went inside the church and found it to be exactly as expected - very quiet and a trifle eerie.

Seeing the unusual raised tomb of Sir Edward Waldegrave in the corner of the church, he took a photograph of it, as he did of a couple of other interesting points that caught his eye.

Outside again, he took two more photographs of the site of the old burnt down Borley Rectory, this left him with a couple of exposures left in the camera, which he used up on his way back to Sudbury.

A few days later, he took the film to be developed and later called to pick up the prints.

To his surprise, the photographs that he had taken both before and after the Borley snaps were perfect, but those taken at Borley were completely blank. The negatives were checked, to prove that the camera shutter had indeed opened, but nothing had been imprinted on the film. A later check on the camera failed to reveal any fault, and it has worked perfectly ever since!!

THE MYSTERIOUS EXPOSURE

As a complete contrast to the previous story, a group of investigators were spending the night outside Borley church and up till 3 a.m. the night had been uneventful, until one of the group had a feeling that 'something' was happening close to the tiny sealed up chancel door. Alerting the rest of the group they all turned their attention on this door but failed to see anything.

The 'feeling' was so strong that they decided to try their luck with a couple of photographs, more in hope than expectancy.

When the film was developed, they were surprised to see what they interpreted to be a large old fashioned chancel door with the outline of what they thought was a veiled bride about to enter.

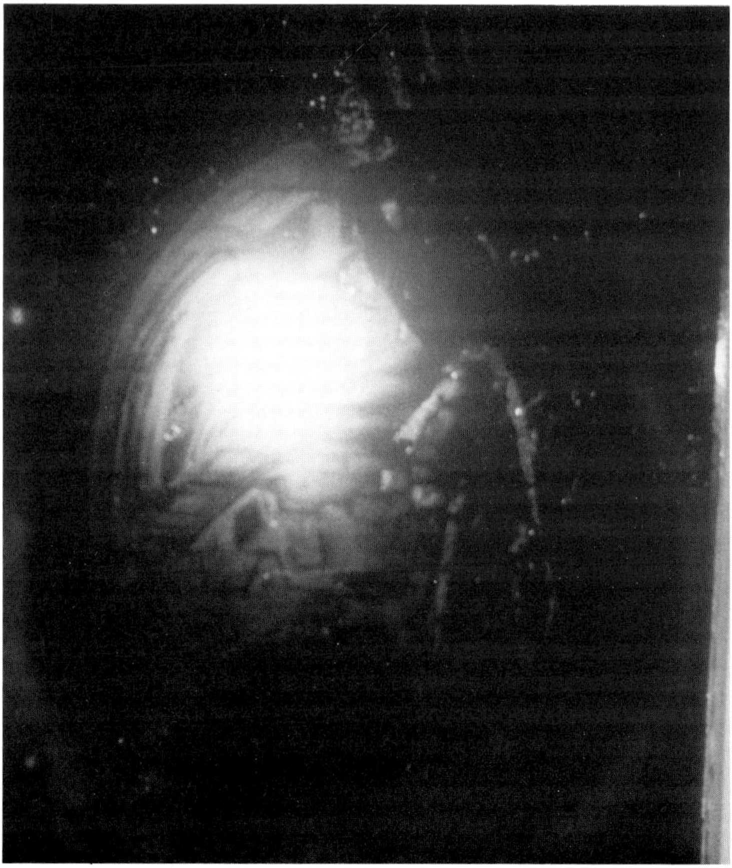

STRANGE HAPPENINGS IN THE 1980's

In the early 1980's, a couple who had moved away from Borley in the 1930's, made a return visit with their twenty-five year's old daughter.

After pointing out to their daughter where 'in their day' the Rectory used to be, they crossed the road and headed towards the church.

As they walked along the path towards the church they all heard the sound of the organ playing Handel's Largo.

They commented how lucky they were to arrive at a time when a rehearsal was in progress, but when they reached the entrance to the porch the music stopped. Thinking that the organist had stopped for a break, they opened the church door and walked in. Looking around they were surprised to find the church completely empty, and to their surprise, the organ consul was closed and locked and there was no sign of the organist!!

Whilst they were looking around the church, they were suddenly pelted with small pebbles coming from above them, looking up, they could see nowhere they could have possibly come from - they decided to leave the church without any more ado.

As they left, they saw a man cutting the grass in the churchyard, walking over to him they told him about the music and the pebbles, without showing any surprise he just remarked that it was some radio programme, and carried on cutting the grass!!

MORE BORLEY STORIES

Borley Rectory Cottage has been reported many times as being haunted, but usually the alleged hauntings have been dismissed as being associated with the infamous Rectory.

However, a little research soon revealed that Rectory Cottage was built early in the 1930's on the site of an old Inn that was demolished in 1799.

Sometime during the 18th century, there had been a murder at the Inn and two coachmen were beheaded. Whether this was one incident or two is not known, nor if there is any possible connection between these two coachmen and the legendary coach driven by two headless coachmen.

Perhaps the haunting at Rectory Cottage has more to do with the past history of the Inn than either the old monastery or Rev Bull's ill-fated rectory.

THE GHOSTLY CHILDREN OF BORLEY SCHOOL

Despite the fact that Borley is considered to be a small village, it is astonishing the large number of places and buildings that are allegedly haunted.

Almost as if not wishing to be upstaged, the local school is said to echo with the sounds of children laughing and shouting at times when there are no children on the premises.

More than once the caretaker has been called out at night when children have been heard crying and passersby thought that perhaps children had been locked in.

THE FACE IN THE WINDOW

Not far from Borley Lodge, there is a 17th century cottage where many people have seen the face of an elderly lady staring from a window, but when waved to, she disappears.

This same cottage also has the reputation of being haunted by a 'Thing' which has been described as an 'embodiment of evil'. However, the residents, understandably, did not wish to discuss the matter.

Maybe more information will become available in the future.

THE HAUNTINGS AT PURKIS FARM

The ancient farmhouse at Purkis Farm on Borley Green was in its prime about the time of the Civil Wars and by all accounts it could well have been in the thick of the fighting at one time.

Many times over the years the sounds of phantom musket shots have been heard both in and around the house and lead musket balls have been found in the grounds.

Inside the house, groans and sighs were quite common at one time as were the shadowy figures that suddenly appeared and then disappeared through the walls.

Outside, the apparition of a cavalier has been seen half running, half stooping, as if trying to scuttle from cover to cover without being seen. Maybe this is the same cavalier who haunts Borley Lodge only a couple of hundred yards away.

BORLEY LODGE

For over two hundred and fifty years this 15th century building is reputed to have been haunted by the ghost of a cavalier.

It is thought he was one of the survivors who fled from the Battle of Nazeby and took refuge at the house of a known sympathiser.

Eventually, Cromwell's men found his hiding place and wasted no time in putting him to death.

Since that fateful day, his ghost has been strolling along the long landing, occasionally stopping to gaze wistfully out of the windows, no doubt as he did so many times in his last few days.

Who this unfortunate man was has always remained a mystery, but there is every chance that he was known to the distant relatives of the present owners whose family have owned Borley Lodge for over 400 years, in fact since before the Reformation.

BORLEY NOTES

A story related by a distant relative of Rev Foyster, tells that it was common knowledge in Cromwellian times that a terrible tragedy occurred at Borley that 'evoked the utmost evil of mankind'.

A Catholic priest named either Dominic or Enoch and a nun were lovers, but their 'master's' found out. The nun was murdered and the priest was nailed to a cross and crucified in Borley church. When he was half dead, some Cromwellian soldiers cut him down and hung him upside down in a nearby well. Three days later the soldiers returned and cut the rope allowing his body to drop into the water.

These same soldiers also stole the church plate, put many villagers to the sword, burnt cottages and threw weighted bodies into a nearby pond.

On face value this seems to be a variation of the legendary nun and monk story, unfortunately the truth will never be known.

****

Farmhands working in the old barn opposite Borley church swear that they have looked out of the open doors and seen about a dozen misty figures pass the barn, cross the road and disappear at the edge of the pond near Borley Place.

****

It is said that three Ley Lines meet under Borley Church, this could possibly account for some of the power there.

****

At times a horrible smell appears in a restricted area near the church, but so far its source has not been traced!!

****

Returning to the question of the possibility of there being two ghostly nuns, this suggestion was reinforced by more sightings by a team. One group observed what appeared to be that of a figure of a young nun in a light green habit, which suggests she was a novice, another group clearly saw an older nun, but she was wearing a dark blue habit!! Both were seen heading for the church.

INVESTIGATORS REPORTS

In the spring of 1961, a small group of paranormal investigators staged an all-night vigil in the vicinity of Borley church. Among the 'happenings' they witnessed and described as "not compatible with a normal explanation", were the sighting of 'blue floating lights' between five and ten feet above ground level when seen from a distance of about thirty feet.

At 3 a.m., voices and footsteps were heard in the lane, but there was no sign of anybody and no one passed the group who were standing on the side of the road.

A strange mal-function of two torches, car headlights and a press photographer's flash camera, all failed simultaneously.

Whilst this was all happening there was a quite noticeable feeling of intense cold and some of the group said that they experienced a feeling of depletion in the vicinity of the churchyard shrubbery.

****

In 1971, one team of investigators carried out what had become a routine operation for them. They had already built up a good relationship with the local residents, also with the caretaker of the church, so much in fact, that they were often loaned the key of the church and allowed to place tape recorders overnight, also on occasions, to stay in the church overnight.

It was on one such occasion that two of the team set up several tape recorders in different areas in the church in order to try to trace various movements. They picked up sounds of footsteps, the sound of a door bolt being moved, the creaking of a door being opened and closed, and the sound of an organ being played. Also whilst the two men were in the church, just sitting and watching, they both saw pin-pricks of light darting about, just like fire flies!

****

Further recordings made in Borley Church in 1985, record what was believed to be animal or humanoid grunts, something like a growl. Other sounds were of gaspings, clumpings and sounds similar to large pieces of wood being knocked together, also scratching sounds and a faint form of chanting.

REPORTS FROM A SURREY BASED TEAM

Early one morning, four of the team were standing by their car outside the church when they heard voices and laughter coming along the road from the direction of Borley School near the river and railway, they described it as sounding just like a garden party!

They jumped into the car and went slowly towards from where they heard the sounds, but there was nothing visible to account for it.

Earlier that night they had left a heavy tape recorder running in the church porch and then they sat in their car outside the church taking it in turns to keep an eye on the porch door. About 2 a.m. they heard a terrific crash in the porch. When they went to see what had caused the noise they found the tape recorder smashed to pieces on the floor and the tape from the spools strewn all over the porch. Nobody was seen to enter the porch and the church door was locked and even if somebody had entered the porch, there was no way they could have got out without being seen, bearing in mind that as soon as the crash was heard, four pairs of eyes never left that door for a second!!

****

Two members of a group were locked in the church at 10 p.m. equipped with various tape recorders and temperature measuring gear. Although there were long periods where no activity was seen, heard or recorded, there were times when several things seemed to happen together. Unfortunately their report did not mention the actual times of the occurrences. But the sequence of events were as follows:-

Heard and recorded bumps near the altar.

Later saw a ghostly figure open a door which does not exist.

Sounds on tape near chancel door.

Temperature dropped, feeling of being watched.

Static on tape also sound of something being dropped, followed by a human sigh.

Second cassette recorder jammed, tape pulled out.

Noises of a bolt on a door being drawn.

****

It is interesting to note the large number of tape recorders that have been damaged either in the porch or inside the church. Sometimes they have been smashed completely, at other times, the tapes or cassettes have been unwound and rendered useless. It would appear that something or someone objects to recordings.

EAST BERGHOLT

STRANGE HAPPENINGS AT THE OLD FRIARY (OLD HALL)

Although still locally known as The Old Friary, but now renamed Old Hall, this gaunt looking building was once known as St Mary's Abbey, a Benedictine nunnery. During the 1939/45 War it was commandeered by the army and occupied by troops and housed both an officers and a sergeants mess. After the war a number of Franciscan Friars occupied it for a few years when it became known as East Bergholt Monastery, but when they left, it remained empty for a while. The next occupants formed a community and by all accounts have successfully been running a commune there ever since.

When it was occupied by the nuns, it had a reputation of being a very cold building and the fact that they belonged to what was regarded as a very 'severe' order did not help matters.

Discipline was very strict, especially for the novices; they had to carry out their duties however sick they may have been and this fact is borne out by the number of graves within the grounds, also by the niches in the narrow corridors where some of their names are recorded.

There was a headline case when one of the nuns managed to escape. She was lucky enough to reach Manningtree railway station late one night after being pursued by the attendants from the nunnery. She owed her freedom to the very sympathetic Station Master who refused to hand her over and gave her shelter for the night and then put her on the early morning train to London. The full story of her escape can be read in her book "The Escaped Nun".

Even in those days, rumours circulated about the various unexplained ghostly happenings inside the building as well as stories of whispy figures having been seen gliding between the nunnery and the burial ground. These persistent tales often made it difficult for the Reverend Mother to get local help when needed.

It was with no great surprise to the locals when, during the war, more stories of the supernatural were related by the troops stationed there.

One such story concerned a door that led to the sergeants mess. Every night at ten minutes to eleven the door would unlatch itself and slowly swing open, followed by a sharp drop in temperature. To make sure that there was no trickery, men were stationed each side of the door a few minutes before the time, but still the door opened on time and nothing was seen. At one time the door was removed, but still the temperature dropped on time and when the door was re-hung it still opened as usual.

Another story related the time when an eighteen year old soldier was lying on his bed one night, when he saw the door that connected with the next room suddenly open and a misty shape enter his room. Paralysed with fear, he felt a pair of ice cold hands placed upon his face; at this he screamed and the shape disappeared. The next morning it was found that his dark head of hair had turned snow white!!

After this event, even the hard hearted army officers were concerned, and they moved the men out of those two rooms and sealed them up.

There was also a passage leading from one of the rear doors into the building and many times the troops claimed that they had seen and felt ghostly shapes along this passage, so much, in fact, that many of them would rather take the long walk around the building to the front entrance rather than risk using that passage.

Even to this day some of the occupants keep a 'weather eye' open when walking along some of the long corridors, and some of the rooms are still sealed off!!

****

EAST BERGHOLT

THE HAUNTED HARE AND HOUNDS INN

The Hare and Hounds public house at East Bergholt is said to have a ghost who is affectionately called Fred.

Fred is quite a character as a ghost, so much in fact that in real life he must have been quite a practical joker. He now likes to flush the cistern in the toilet, runs up and down the stairs, slams doors, moves chairs in the bar in full view of the customers, and to show his strength, he even lifted one customer bodily off the floor.

PENTLOW

THE PENTLOW FOLLY

There was a period in our past history when wealthy people were able to indulge in the luxury of being able to put their money into satisfying their whims, by building 'follies'.

These buildings, sometimes took the form of grotesque structures, memorials, inland lighthouses, grottoes, towers etc.

In fact, there are enough of these strange buildings in existence for a group of people to form 'The Folly Club' and spend quite a large amount of their leisure time visiting various locations in this country.

At Pentlow, the 'folly' is in the form of an octagonal, crenellated tower some sixty feet high. It was built in 1858 by Reverend Edward Bull as a memorial to his parents, although the locals prefer to tell strangers that it was built by a crazy land owner who would climb to the top, so that he could watch his workers to make sure that they didn't waste his time.

It is just perhaps a coincidence that the Rev Edward Bull, also happened to be the father and grandfather of those other eccentric clerics of Borley, the Rev Henry and Rev Harry Bull!!

One day in 1992, two members of the 'Folly Club', a husband and wife, decided to visit Pentlow.

Leaving their car on the road, they made their way on foot to the tower. After looking round the outside of the building they went inside. The ground floor consisted of a single room with a stone stairway leading to the higher parts.

The man declined to go up the stairs, because he was unable to withstand heights and elected to stay in the lower room, whilst his wife went to the top to see the view.

Some minutes after his wife had left him, he was overcome by a terrible feeling of oppression. He later related that the feeling was so intense that he went outside because he could no longer stand it, and said that although he did not believe in ghosts, he felt that there was something evil in the tower.

A few minutes later his wife came running from the tower in a panic, so much so, that she did not see her husband standing to one side, and ran straight back to their car.

The husband ran after her, wondering what was the matter. When he eventually managed to calm her down, she told him that when she was just over half way up the tower, she thought that he had changed his mind and decided to follow her, she could hear laboured breathing a little way behind her and decided to wait for him.

As the breathing got nearer she suddenly felt very cold, then felt what appeared to be cold clammy hands feeling her face then moving down her body. She screamed and ran down the stairs as fast as she could and was convinced that she heard an old man's coarse laugh behind her!!

RIDGEWELL

THE AIRFIELD GHOSTS

During World War II, a large area of Ridgewell and parts of nearby villages were flattened to form an American Air Base, the home of the 381st Bomb Group, USAAF.

No sooner had the airfield been completed than the first planes' began to arrive. Suddenly the skies became alive with these huge aircraft. Flying direct from America they landed on this brand new base that was to be their home for the next few years.

Within a few weeks they were fully operational and started making daily raids over France, then later into Germany.

Nearly all of their raids were in daylight, dozens of them taking off, day in and day out, at 6.30 a.m. So regular in fact, that the local residents didn't use alarm clocks to wake up, the noise from the engines being warmed up and the Jeeps tearing about were sufficient, and in the winter months it was not only the noise but the bright arc lights that seemed to be everywhere.

Years after the war, the local residents still claim that they see ghostly lights across the derelict airfield and hear the shouts of the airmen, the revving Jeep engines, and the sounds of returning aircraft tyres screeching on the tarmac. Some people claim to hear the occasional crash of a badly shot up 'plane that has made it back to base, but was unable to get its undercarriage down.

Very little remains now-a-days of the airfield apart from a few rusting Nissen huts and the mortuary.

Yes, you've guessed it. Ghosts of the brave American airmen whose mangled remains have rested in there are often seen wandering in the vicinity.

STOKE-BY-NAYLAND

THORINGTON HALL

Built in the early seventeenth-century Thorington Hall, Stoke-by-Nayland, Suffolk, situated on the Essex/Suffolk border, overlooks John Constable's Stour Valley and Dedham Vale, the beauty of which was immortalised by the then young brilliant artist.

Thorington Hall, now in the care of the National Trust, has several features that draws the attention of all types of visitor.

From the outside, it appears as a typical seventeenth-century Suffolk merchants residence, oak-framed and plastered walls with a hand-made peg tile roof, topped by a magnificent six flue chimney stack consisting of six individual octagonal flues towering up to some fifty feet.

Internally, the rooms are equally impressive, the main living-room has an ornamented plaster surround and in 1937 when the plasterwork was being repaired, behind the plaster the builders discovered a lady's shoe. This was removed and taken to the Colchester Museum where it was dated as being sixteenth-century. The shoe is still on display in the Museum.

There is an interesting point about having a shoe buried within the walls of a house. In Elizabethan days it was quite common to build items made of leather into a building as a form of protection against ghosts and evil spirits.

This gives rise to the possibility of there having been a haunting here from the early days. In fact the house has been haunted for many years by at least two separate ghosts, one being a little girl wearing a plain brown dress tied around the waist with a chord, who has been seen and heard many times over the years walking slowly along the dark landing at the top of the stairs.

It is thought that she was a child from the Umfreville family who once lived there, although there do not seem to be any surviving records of the death of such a child here.

The other ghost seems to be that of a heavily built man whose heavy footsteps have often been heard climbing up and down the stairs, also moving across several of the upstairs rooms.

In the early days, the upper rooms of the house - probably used to accommodate domestic staff - were reached by ladders from a passage, but about 1650 an oak staircase was installed. The newel posts were beautifully carved, this being an unusual feature for an upper staircase, but on the third newel from the bottom there is an unusual builders mark of three interlacing circles. Here again, three interlacing circles were thought at one time to have a magical significance relating to ghosts. It is in the area of this staircase that the little girl has mostly been seen, also where the heavy footsteps are heard!!

Just after the 1939/45 war a group of visiting American tourists were visiting Thorington Hall when a cupboard door swung open on its own volition and a human pelvic bone fell to the floor. Enquiries revealed that the bone had not been seen in the house before, also tests on it revealed that it was well over two hundred years old!!

MISTLEY

THE GHOST OF MATTHEW HOPKINS, WITCH-FINDER GENERAL

Once the most hated and feared man in Essex and Suffolk, Matthew Hopkins, the self styled Witch-finder General had his headquarters in Manningtree and Mistley and is thought to return to the scenes of his 'crimes'.

Rooms in Mistley's Thorn Hotel, once used for his office, are said to still be visited by his ghost.

In recent years many fishermen of all ages, fishing in the large lake in the grounds of Mistley Place, have been startled by the sudden appearance of the figure of a man standing little over five feet in height, wearing old fashioned clothes and a tall hat, and knee high boots. This description fits Matthew Hopkins exactly.

This figure is reported to have been seen at least ten times between 1991 and 1993, often by two or more people at a time.

One 6ft 2in, fearless twenty-two years old man, a very experienced night fisherman, reported that one night the figure suddenly manifested in the bright moonlight within ten feet of himself and a companion. The figure remained stationary for about 30 seconds then began to drift towards them; at this move, the fisherman swung his fishing rod round and the end joint passed right through the figure, at which both of them turned and ran, only returning the next morning to retrieve their gear.

It is said that Matthew Hopkins' ghost also returns to two public houses in Manningtree where he used to interrogate some of his victims.

MISTLEY

THE HAUNTED TERRACE

Mistley seems to abound with stories of hauntings, some have friendly ghosts, some mischievous, others have apparitions appearing for seemingly unknown reasons and occasionally there are cases of manifestations with rather bizarre connections.

Nearly opposite Mistley's famous Robert Adam Swan Fountain and pond, there is a terrace of 18/19th century houses. Legend has it that every other house has its own ghostly story.

One house has a particularly bizarre story associated with it. Not too many years ago a couple were said to have moved in with an elderly gentleman who owned the house, whereby they had free accommodation in return for giving care and attention to the old man.

For a while all went well, but then the couple started to neglect their 'duties'. Through the lack of care the old gentleman rapidly deteriorated and became bedridden. Medical attention was denied him, as was sufficient food.

One day when the couple were out, a lady was passing the house when she heard a weak voice from one of the upper room windows "Help me, help me". Looking up, she saw the pale face of a very old man at the window.

Not wishing to get involved in other peoples affairs, she carried on walking. Maybe her conscience troubled her, because later she told a friend what she had heard and seen. This friend informed the authorities and a social worker called at the house.

To the horror of the social worker she found a weak, emaciated old man, old before his years, his finger and toe nails had grown so long that they had curled over and had doubled back into the skin.

A few days later he died, and the infamous couple disappeared overnight without trace.

In due course the house was let to new tenants. Not being aware of the past events in the house, they were surprised one evening to see the figure of an old man appear from an upstairs bedroom feebly making his way along the landing only to disappear on the top of the stairs.

At other times they distinctly heard sighs and moans coming from the same bedroom, often followed by weak cries for help!!

MANNINGTREE

THE SPIRIT THAT MOVED ON

Manningtree's Red Lion public house in South Street, used to have a jovial looking ghost who was given the nickname of 'George'. His favourite party trick was to appear in the club room dressed in Victorian clothes, and a former landlady was startled one night when she went into this room to find 'George' standing there, as large as life. He appeared to be equally startled, but seemed so friendly that she was not afraid. Sadly George has left the Red Lion for his spirits elsewhere, — he was exorcised.

****

THE VANISHING ISLAND

In the grounds of a large house on the Essex/Suffolk border, there is a well stocked lake; the owners from time to time have fishing parties and occasionally allow the estate employees and their families to enjoy a day out, fishing.

It was on such a day that a young man was fishing from the bank of the lake, when he was suddenly aware of another man fishing from a small island. Until then, he was not aware that there was an island, but thinking to himself that there are lots of things one takes for granted until something in particular draws attention to it, he carried on fishing.

After a while, he began to wonder how the man had got on to the island, so he called out and asked him, but the old angler just waved, laughed and carried on with his fishing.

Soon after this, the boy was astonished to see a mist appearing around the edge of the island, then the whole island, man, fishing rods and all, began to sink slowly into the lake hardly causing a ripple!!

In case the reader feels that this is just another 'fisherman's yarn', other people have also had a similar experience there.

The estate management requested that the location should not be revealed because the lake is strictly private property.

POLSTEAD

THE RED BARN DREAM

Mention the names of Maria Marten, William Corder or even the Red Barn, around the little Suffolk village of Polstead and many people within hearing distance will turn and walk away.

One might well wonder the reason and the answer is simple. For over onc hundred and sixty years the local residents have been trying to live down the unwanted publicity their once quiet and sleepy village attracted, when a murder was committed.

It all started in 1827 when a young Polstead girl, Maria Marten, fell in love with William Corder, the son of a wealthy local farmer.

Really, it was a twist of the old tale; a simple village maiden, believing that her future would be assured if she allowed the rich farmer's son to have his way with her, and talk of marriage.

William Corder however, never had any intention of marrying Maria, although he enticed her into one of his father's barns, the Red Barn, with the promise of taking her to Ipswich and getting married, that was on 18th May 1827. That was the last time Maria was seen alive.

When she failed to return home that night her mother contacted William who told her that Maria had gone to Ipswich to get some things for their wedding.

The next day he left the village for London from where he later wrote to Maria's mother saying that Maria and he were married and were living together.

This would have seemed to have been the end of the matter, but some eleven months later no further news of her daughter was received.

Then, three nights running, Maria's mother had a recurring dream. It was so realistic that she felt that someone or something was giving her the message that Maria had been murdered and buried in the corner of the Red Barn.

The dream was so compelling that she persuaded her husband to go to the barn with the farm bailiff and investigate. There they found the rotting remains of Maria's body in a shallow grave.

William Corder was traced living in London, where he was accused and arrested for the murder of Maria Marten. He later made a full confession, a crime for which he paid with his life.

POLSTEAD

POLSTEAD RECTORY

There are many Suffolk rectories with a long history of being haunted, and Polstead is no exception.

Despite having an exorcism service performed many years ago, Polstead Rectory is still said to be haunted and in 1978 the disturbances were sufficient to send the rector and his wife running to a nearby neighbour for help because they felt unable to spend another night in the Rectory.

The Rev. Hayden Foster told his neighbours that his wife Margot, had experienced what she explained as an attempt by some unknown force to strangle her and for some time they had been troubled by strange noises and eerie feelings and things were not getting any better.

The previous rector had also been troubled in his short sojourn there and he had packed up and returned to his native Ireland.

Even before the occupancy of these two rectors, there were stories circulating around the village of ghostly 'happenings' in the Rectory. Although it was not officially recorded as being the reason for other rectors leaving after only relatively short periods, the local villagers with a nod and a wink knew the reason.

ASHINGDON

GHOSTS OF AN ANCIENT BATTLE

This corner of Essex has a reputation of being one of the most haunted districts in the county.

It was the scene of one of the bloodiest battles between the Anglo-Saxon English and the Danish invaders and the hill upon which the church stands overlooking the low lying battle ground has an unusual tradition that no grass will ever grow on that field where so much blood was spilt. Over the years, on quiet windless evenings, people passing this spot have frequently heard eerie sounds of moaning and cries as of from the wounded and dying.

There is a lane which winds its way past the church and the old battle field. This lane, according to local belief, has its own claim to being haunted. A woman hanged herself from one of the trees, and it is said that her cries could still be heard for some years even after the trees had been cut down and to make matters worse, these cries seemed to follow one for hours.

DEDHAM

THE SWEEPS BOY

An unusual story was related by a man whose daughter had lived in a cottage in Brook Street, Dedham.

After living happily in the cottage for about six months with her husband and five year old daughter, they began to notice a gradual change in the little girl's behaviour. She had always been a cheerful child, but her laughter and smiling face suddenly changed to outbreaks of tears with long periods of silence.

The worried parents took her to the doctor for a check up, but nothing was found to be physically amiss. The doctor came to the conclusion that there was some other reason, possibly psychological.

One day, whilst waiting for an appointment with a specialist, the child suddenly burst into tears and started screaming, then without warning she ran to the open living-room window and climbed out.

The startled mother ran after her and just managed to catch her as she neared the gate. With great difficulty she managed to drag the still screaming child back into the house.

Eventually calming the girl down, her mother tried to find out what had upset her so. Still very weepy, the child said it was the boy, the boy with the black face. She said that she had often seen him in the living-room and he always spoke to her, but today he chased her and when she went to smack him, her hand went right through him and he disappeared.

The mother quickly realised that her daughter had seen a ghost and began to ask neighbours if they knew anything about the cottage being haunted, but none did, until however, one elderly lady remembered that some years ago there had been a rumour that there was a history of the place being haunted.

Apparently many years ago, at the time when chimney sweeps used young boys to climb up into the chimney to clean down the soot, such a lad was suffocated up the living-room flue and from time to time his ghost had been seen in that room, but always only by young children.

Needless to say, the house was soon put up for sale and the family moved out. The little girl? Well, although she is now a young woman, wild horses would not drag her to Dedham again.

LONG MELFORD

THE MYSTERIES AND HAPPENINGS AT THE BULL HOTEL

This 15th century building, once a wealthy wool merchant's residence before becoming a coaching hostelry, has a history of mystery, murder and haunting dating back many years.

Sometime in the 17th century, a man was stabbed to death in the porch of the hotel. His body was taken upstairs and placed in a bedroom overnight, but the next morning, when the undertakers arrived with the coffin, the body was missing.

Many times over the years, occupiers of this room have complained that it is haunted and have asked to be moved to another room, or have packed up and left.

Measuring along the passage outside this bedroom and measuring the inside, it immediately becomes apparent that there must be a sealed up room between the bedroom and the en suite bathroom. Could this possibly have any connection with the past mystery??

One day, downstairs in the bar, customers were startled to see a copper pot rise about two inches above a shelf behind the bar then slowly move horizontally for about three feet, then float slowly to the floor.

Similar things have happened in the kitchen many times, mostly in slow motion, usually when there is someone present.

Other objects move of their own volition, and some disappear and reappear days later, even the dining room chairs get rearranged overnight.

Despite these minor incidents, the management and staff more than compensate with their friendliness and willingness to please and the food is equal to any.

NAYLAND

THE HAUNTED WHITE HART HOTEL

The old White Hart Hotel at Nayland, near Colchester, is reputedly haunted by the restless spirit of a woman who, it is said, was killed by a soldier over two hundred years ago.

Staff and guests have seen her small forlorn figure standing at the top of the stairs and sometimes in one of the bedrooms.

Maybe she is still searching for her killer - "Hell hath no wrath like a woman scorned"!!

IPSWICH

THE GHOSTS OF COWELL'S FACTORY

For many years the old established firm of W. S. Cowell & Company, until the buildings were demolished to make way for the new shopping Mall, had their factory in Ipswich's Butter Market.

The factory was built over the ruins of an old monastery, so it is not surprising that over the years the ghostly apparitions of monks have many times been seen in and around the vicinity of the factory.

There were at least two occasions when young women employees fainted after becoming aware of an old monk standing looking at them and then fading away as soon as they screamed.

Working one night inside the factory, a burly Irish labourer also saw the figure of a monk slowly gliding towards him. Despite his size, he broke into a cold sweat and trembled all over, but when the monk suddenly disappeared only a few feet from him, that was the last straw, he let out an almighty yell and spun round and ran as fast as his rubbery legs would carry him, leaving his coat behind.

The shock was so great that he refused to go back to the factory even to collect his coat and wages.

Other workers also had various experiences over the years. One man with over twenty years service in the factory related how he had seen ghostly shapes many times, also when on night work he had heard footsteps on numerous occasions, but when he investigated, there was no one in the vicinity from where the sounds came from.

One day the same man was working in a different area of the factory when he discovered a steel door set flush with the floor. Being an inquisitive person, he got a crowbar and prised the heavy door open and to his surprise, found a flight of stone steps that led into a tunnel which was sealed up a few yards from the entrance. The general appearance of the tunnel suggested that the iron door had not been opened for many, many, years and one is left wondering why indeed the tunnel was built and where did it originally lead to? Was it a part of the old monastery?

Builders carrying out some alterations, discovered a sealed underground chamber containing several skeletons. It did not appear to have been a burial chamber as such, the positions of the skeletons suggested they had not been placed there, but rather thrown, or even perhaps, people had been incarcerated and had struggled to get out. However, by the condition of the bones, they had been there for many years.

When the site was being cleared prior to the building of the shopping Mall, workmen discovered what was believed to have been the old monastery well of very great depth. Tragically, the well was filled in with rubbish instead of being cleaned out and preserved. Who knows just what might have been revealed had it been, after all, when King Henry VIII dissolved the monasteries most of the valuables were hurriedly dumped down the wells.

Also, bearing in mind that Ipswich was the home town of the infamous Cardinal Wolsey, the monks would not have had much time to find a safer hiding place in which to dispose of the gold ornaments etc.

GT. OAKLEY

THE HAUNTED MAYBUSH INN

The Maybush Inn at Gt. Oakley is said to have been the site of an unusual haunting - a ghost who liked playing marbles. Sounds of marbles being rolled across an upstairs floor have been heard many times, also the sounds of objects falling, followed by footsteps crossing the floor.

There have also been reports of a ghostly oriental lady having been seen gliding from room to room then just fading away.

These reports date back to the 1970's when the landlord of the time disregarded the tales his customers told him of earlier 'happenings', and flatly refused to believe in such things as ghosts and hauntings especially in his pub - that was until one night when he heard something definitely rolling across the bedroom floor, he then agreed that it could possibly have been the phantom marble player; but was finally converted when he actually saw the small slim figure of a young woman dressed in a kimono crossing his bedroom to disappear through the wall, only to reappear a minute or so latter appearing to be carrying an object in front of her; she crossed the room and faded away just before reaching the outside wall!!

In January 1993 a visit was made by a researcher to see if any further activity had taken place, but the landlord and his wife both said that although they had lived there for the past nine years, they were unaware of anything unusual, although at times they have heard odd creaks etc. but what eise would you expect from an old timber framed building??

NEEDHAM MARKET

THE GHOSTS OF CORPSE WAY

'Corpse Way'! 'Corpse Way'!! Many roads are aptly named, usually for a very good reason, e.g. Church Road, Chapel Lane, School Lane, etc. etc. But to call the road that leads to the cemetery 'Corpse Way' somehow feels like being hit below the belt.

Maybe that is just how the spirits of some of those who have been buried in the village cemetery feel, and, in protest, are making their feelings felt by manifesting at odd times along that leafy lane.

A local man was walking along Corpse Way one day in 1990, when he was suddenly aware of a lady, dressed in blue, walking in the same direction about fifty yards ahead of him. Thinking it strange that he hadn't noticed her earlier, but having been deep in thought, he put it down to that, and carried on.

As he approached a bend in the lane he lost sight of the lady and thought that she must have walked a little faster than he and had crossed to the other side of the road allowing her to be obscured by the bend. However, when he reached the bend himself, there was no sign of her and although the road was perfectly straight for nearly half a mile, and there was certainly no gateways or anywhere for her to have turned off.

His only conclusion was that he must have seen a ghost.

The same man related his story to the local lady librarian. She remarked how strange it was that not long ago her husband also had an unusual experience on the corner of that same lane.

Late one evening he was passing the end of Corpse Way, when he clearly saw a policeman standing there. Not thinking much about it he carried on walking, but after a few yards it dawned on him that there was something rather odd. He turned round to have a second look at him but he had disappeared.

It was only then that he realised that the policeman was wearing an old Victorian type uniform.

NEEDHAM MARKET

'SPIRITS' IN THE OLD WAGON AND HORSES

As with so many local public houses nowadays, the time comes when trade diminishes and the cost of updating and refurbishing becomes so uneconomical that the brewers tend to cut their losses and sell off the properties for private occupation.

Such was the fate of Needham's old Wagon and Horses public house, but being a fair sized building, it was divided into two properties, one called 'The Wagon', the other 'The Horses', thus the old name was retained.

An American couple leased 'The Wagon' for a period, and at one stage advertised for a baby sitter for a few evenings each week.

One young lady who applied for the job was asked if she was at all nervous as the ghost of an old lady was frequently seen wandering about the house. Not wishing to show any fear or belief in ghosts she took the job, but after the first night she failed to turn up for further work and didn't even come back for her wages!!

Since this incident there have been many tenants in The Wagon, none of them staying very long.

'The Horses'? Well, for a period that was occupied by an elderly blind couple who could not see anything anyway!

ACTON

THE LEGEND OF ACTON PLACE

For many years, legend has it that a ghostly death-coach, driven by a headless coachman, pounds along the narrow lane leading to the ruins of Acton Place. As it reaches the gates leading to the long drive, it suddenly vanishes into thin air.

Acton Place, the residence of that famous, legendary, eighteenth-century miser Robert Jennens, once reputed to have been the richest man in England, who was in fact such an eccentric that he chose to live in the cellar of his magnificent mansion and dress in rags rather than wear any of the large wardrobe of clothes he had accumulated in earlier years.

Maybe this legend started through his meanness, or, as one local explained "the devil came to claim his own"!!

ROWHEDGE

DEJA VU

The following story was received and considered to be so unusual that it just had to be included in this book.

Returning to England after living abroad for some years, Veronica spent some time searching for a suitable property. One day she found a cottage to which she was drawn to even before she went inside; somehow she knew this was "it". She immediately named it 'Deja vu', just why she didn't know. It was just as she had seen it so many times in her dreams.

Moving in, she furnished the place to make it look and feel warm and inviting but, somehow at times, it had that strange unreal "feel" about it. Often, when all was silent, she sensed that some-one was watching her.

One evening she was entertaining some friends when they all heard a noise coming from the top of the stairs. Veronica, seeing her guests were startled, said "Don't worry, it's only Hepzibah".

Later, when her friends had left, she puzzled over why she had called the 'presence' 'Hepzibah' - what did it mean?

During the two years Veronica had lived in the cottage, she felt the "feeling" getting stronger and stronger - the sense that it was a woman watching her - frightening, but somehow half-reassuring, almost as if she were watching herself.

The presence of 'Hepzibah' was often felt before bad news or unforeseen illness occurred, as happened the night before a small fire occurred in the cottage.

Veronica began to accept 'Hepzibah' as a friend - a friend she had met and knew intimately at one stage but couldn't recall how; she also felt 'Hepzibah' was trying to convey something to her.

It was a dank November afternoon as Veronica walked her dog. Reluctantly she had left the warm cosy Victorian cottage and strolled across the fields and into the woods close to the riverside village she felt she knew so well, although she seldom walked this way.

The path through the woods led to the village cemetery. Her dog somehow seemed to be leading her and she just followed until, reaching a small wooden gate she unlatched it and walked around the gravestones, the dog pulling eagerly ahead.

Veronica stopped, as if compelled to do so; she was facing a rather ornate headstone engraved with the words “Hepzibah Miller. 1901-1937”. She shuddered, memorised the dates and, pulling the collar of her coat closely about her, hurried home.

Back inside the cottage Veronica drew the curtains, switched on the lamp and looked around - everything appeared as normal. “Hepzibah”, she called, “if you have a message for me, please tell me”, - - - - nothing stirred.

That night Veronica had a dream in which ‘Hepzibah’ came and told her that if she wondered how she knew the river, woods and fields so well it was because she had been there before - - Deja vu - a feeling of having experienced the present situation before - a reminder of her previous incarnation.

A week later Veronica examined the Parish Records. Hepzibah Miller had in fact lived and died in her cottage!!!

****

BRANTHAM

THE HAUNTED BULL INN

The Bull Inn at Brantham, just over the Suffolk border, is said to be haunted by a ghost that likes to be behind the bar.

One night, just before closing time, a barmaid saw a vague form manifesting at the far end of the bar, not wishing to be considered brave, she screamed and ran into the kitchen.

Others working in the bar, including the landlord’s daughter, have experienced the sensation of somebody or something passing them whilst serving customers, usually preceded by cool draught.

One may be forgiven for thinking that being behind the bar is the correct place for spirits!!

CAPEL ST. MARY

A STRANGE VISITATION

On the outskirts of Capel St. Mary, just off the A12 road to Ipswich, there was an unusual visitation concerning an old house on the edge of a wood.

The house, having been derelict for some length of time, had been purchased by a London barrister who, throughout the spring and summer spent all his weekends and spare time carrying out renovations and repairs.

By late summer, he had some of the rooms ready and to do a few last minute jobs, he travelled down on the Friday afternoon and the family were to follow the next day.

Having worked late into the evening, he had just retired for the night, when he was surprised to hear his name being called out quite clearly. Thinking that his family had decided to come down early in order to give him a surprise, he switched on the lights and went downstairs to open the back door, fully expecting to see his wife and family standing on the doorstep, but to his surprise and dismay there was no one there.

He called out. but getting no reply, he started to return to his bedroom. As he reached the bedroom door, his attention was drawn to the open trapdoor in the ceiling, where he had been working earlier and had not replaced the cover. He was flabbergasted to see a small figure of a man who appeared to be about two feet in height, sitting on the trapdoor frame - there he was as large as life, just sitting there swinging his legs backwards and forwards. He was dressed in a brown knicker-bocker suit with braces, a green shirt, boots with stockings up to his knees and on his head a small trilby type hat. He sat there for what seemed a couple of minutes then just disappeared!!

The barrister swore that every word of this story was true and there was certainly no question of him imagining the whole thing, nor had he been drinking!!

Local research revealed that earlier occupiers had often claimed to have seen 'fairies and hob-goblins' about the house and garden, but as they were regarded as being a 'queer' family, nobody believed them!!!

WALTON-ON-THE-NAZE

THE FISHERMAN'S TALE

A man who regularly fished from the end of Walton Pier, was sitting in his usual position just beyond a little hut that served as a shelter at the terminal of the Pier Railway.

Over a period of time he had become familiar with most of the local fishing enthusiasts, but on this occasion he was joined by a man whom he did not recognise.

The stranger, having cast his lines, proceeded to tidy up his equipment and sat down to study the surrounding sea.

After a while, he got up and had a short walk-about and on returning, checked his lines, then went over to have a chat with our man.

Talking about things in general as fishermen will, the stranger lit a cigarette and continued to chat away with quite a strong local accent.

Our man's eyes were drawn to the stranger's thigh length waders, they were made of soft black leather, slightly wrinkled, he had never seen the like before. Then he realised that the rest of the stranger's clothing was definitely unusual, in fact, old fashioned - but there, fishermen often wore strange clothes as a protection against the wind and rain in pursuit of their chosen sport.

After some ten minutes, the stranger returned to his rods and sat down. Our man, reeled in his lines, checked the bait and re-cast. Looking over to where the stranger was sitting, he was astonished to find nobody there, no sign of the man or his gear. Looking along the pier there was not a soul in sight and bearing in mind that the pier is almost a mile long in a straight line, if anyone had walked along it they would have been in sight for at least twenty minutes, and it certainly had not been that length of time since they had been talking!!

****

THE HAUNTED SUN HOTEL

The Sun Hotel at Dedham, is said to be haunted by the ghost of a serving wench whose remains were alleged to have been buried in the garden at the rear of the hotel after she was burnt as a witch. Her misty form is reputed to appear when a disaster is imminent.

WALTON-ON-THE-NAZE

THE MYSTERY ON THE BEACH

A strange story was related by a Walton man who was informed by an acquaintance that the previous evening he was walking his dog along the promenade to the west of the Pier; the tide was out a long way allowing an unusual amount of beach to be visible.

From a distance of some two or three hundred yards he saw a number of figures, there could well have been a dozen or so, near the waters edge, and they appeared to be stooping or bending over something.

After a short while they moved off as a group towards the cliffs, appearing to be carrying something between them. The observer was mystified at what he had just witnessed, nothing was very clear, the figures were hazy, but he thought this was due to the bad visibility caused by a heavy low cloud.

During the whole of this time his dog was very restless and kept pulling him back, whereas normally it would have been pulling forward.

The mysterious figures gradually disappeared against the background of the cliffs and the man returned home still very puzzled.

However, the next day he told his friend of his experience and they agreed to meet that evening and take both their dogs along the same area to see if anything similar occurred.

At the agreed time they duly met and walked along the apparently deserted beach and after walking for some time, they both saw a few shadowy figures moving in the distance, again they seemed to move from the waterline towards the cliffs where they appeared to fade away.

This time there was no reaction from either of the dogs. The same exercise was repeated for the next few nights but nothing further was seen.

A little research revealed that the general area where the figures had been seen might possibly have been the site of the long lost Old Walton church and its graveyard that had been washed out to sea many years ago when severe storms had lashed this coast eroding the cliffs which collapsed into the sea.

Could it have been the ghosts of long dead villagers retrieving their earthly remains??

HARWICH

THE ELECTRICIANS SHOCK

An electrician related the strange and ghostly happenings he witnessed whilst working in the cellar of a Georgian house in Harwich.

In the 1960's, two electricians were given the task to replace the main electric cable from the road to the meter position in the cellar of the house.

Other tradesmen were also working in the house at the same time, but mainly in the upper rooms.

The two electricians were working in the cellar one morning when a carpenter came into the room and hung his dinner bag on a hook on the wall and went back upstairs.

The electricians, busy with their own problems didn't take too much notice of the man or the bag, until a few minutes later they saw the bag lift itself off the hook and slowly float across the cellar and loop itself over another hook in the opposite wall.

Not believing what they had just seen, one of them went over to the bag, lifted it off the hook and carried it back to the original hook, where it remained.

At lunch time, the electricians went outside to their van and brewed a pot of tea. A few minutes later their peace was shattered by an almighty scream from the house, followed by the carpenter falling headlong down the front door steps.

Hurriedly picking himself up, he ran to the van mumbling unintelligibly. The electricians helped him into the van and tried to calm him down with a cup of strong tea which, after a while, he gratefully accepted.

When at last he stopped trembling he explained to them what it was that had frightened him so much. He said that he went down into the cellar to get his lunch and was just about to get hold of his bag, when it jumped off the hook and flew around the cellar at high speed and as he ran up the stairs it followed him; the rest the two men had witnessed.

The carpenter said that under no circumstances would he go back into that house again!!

FELIXSTOWE

THE MYSTERY OF THE PILOT

A most unusual story was related about a World War Two pilot who liked to hitch rides in a car to Ipswich and back.

Just a few years ago a Felixstowe man obtained employment in Ipswich which meant he had to travel by car to and from his home at regular times.

About a month after starting his job, his starting time was altered to a half an hour earlier, an arrangement which suited him as it meant he would avoid the early morning rush.

Setting off on the first day of this new time, he made good progress until he came to the cross roads where traffic was controlled by lights. Being forced to wait until the lights changed, he was musing to himself what a difference that half an hour made when the lights changed to green and off he went.

He had only travelled a couple of hundred yards when he clearly heard whistling in the back of his car and looking in his inside mirror, he was startled to see the figure of an R.A.F. Officer calmly sitting on the back seat merrily whistling away.

Hastily pulling to the side of the road and stopping, he jumped out and opened the rear door. The figure, dressed in a World War Two pilot's leather flying jacket, seemed completely oblivious of the driver asking him what he thought he was doing there.

Badly shaken, the driver jumped back into the car and continued his journey to work, the pilot still whistling away in the back. Parking his car he ran into the factory.

All day he worried about the incident, but dared not tell anyone for fear of ridicule. When his shift finished he hesitatingly walked to his car, looking inside he was relieved to find there was no sign of his uninvited passenger.

Starting the car he headed for Felixstowe, but had only travelled about half a mile when once again he heard the same tune being whistled, there was the pilot again as cool as you like on the back seat.

This time the driver did not stop. but drove as fast as he could towards home, all the time his passenger carried on with the same tune until once again the car was held up by the same traffic lights at the crossroads, then the whistling suddenly stopped and the figure disappeared.

Every day for the rest of that week the unwanted passenger appeared on the back seat just past the crossroads and disappeared there on the return journey.

All this was getting the poor driver down, day in and day out, always the same tune, it was driving him mad, he felt if only the figure would talk or even do something he could endure it, but just to sit there whistling that same tune. No. he had to do something about it, but what.

Over the next weekend he had an idea, he would take a different route, even if it did mean going out of his way by some five miles, but it could be well worth it.

Monday morning came and he took the new route - success, there was no sign of the whistling ghost, at last he felt free.

For a month he kept to this route, but curiously he wondered what would happen if he went the old way. So one day he took the risk and used the main road. Approaching the crossroads with some apprehension, the lights were green, so feeling that the next few yards would tell, he put his foot down and sped across. To his relief, there was no whistle coming from the back, but suddenly he found himself starting to whistle that very same tune. The pilot was never seen again, but the driver found himself haunted by that tune for months.

LANGHAM
GHOSTS IN THE APPLE ORCHARD

During the 1939/45 war, most of the parish of Langham was taken over by the Government and transformed into a large base for the American Army Air Force.

From 1941 to 1944, hundreds of American fighters and bombers operated from this base, carrying out raids over the continent and deep into Germany.

They suffered very heavy losses on these raids, mainly because they were carried out in daylight and most of their targets were in areas heavily defended by enemy fighters and anti-aircraft guns.

It was not unusual to see badly damaged bombers limping home on two of their four engines, only to crash on landing, often killing the surviving members of the crew.

After the war, the concrete runways were broken up and most of the old airfield became a large apple orchard, but there have been many reports of sounds of invisible aircraft swishing low over the trees followed by a sickening crump of metal hitting the ground.

Women pruning the apple trees have frequently reported seeing ghostly American airmen in flying suits, wandering as if lost amongst the trees, some appearing to be badly wounded, but when approached they disappear.

WIVENHOE

THE HAUNTED 'GREYHOUND'

Years ago, Wivenhoe was a small fishing village on the River Colne, with a thriving boat yard. Through hard work, coupled with a good quality of the fish and the excellence of the boats produced, the village quickly grew into a small town.

As the town became more prosperous and attracted more people and businesses, so did it attract the less desirable elements - smugglers, robbers and even murderers.

Wivenhoe, as with many other small coastal towns, also had more than its share of public ale houses per head of population, but now, perhaps sadly, many have closed down and some even demolished.

One pub that still remains in High Street is the Greyhound, parts of which are thought to be 14th century, the rest - old, but not so old as the rear section that used to be the kitchen but is now a 'club' room.

An inn as old as this is expected to have its ghosts, and it does not disappoint you. A mischievous poltergeist likes to hide the various pub keys, but they always seem to turn up later in a different place. One of the two landladies thought that she would put a stop to its little games by chaining all the keys together and hanging them from a hook behind the bar, but what happens - keys and chain disappear!

Perhaps it is the same playful ghost who from time to time removes and hides other small items from the bars, also there was an occasion when the caretaker, alone in the building with all windows and external doors locked, had collected a number of plastic bags into a heap on the bar floor. Suddenly, one of the bags rose out from the middle of the heap, floated across the room for a distance of some ten feet at a height of about three feet, then dropped to the floor. The startled caretaker nervously went over to it and returned it to the heep, where it remained until taken away.

Whilst she was in the staff toilet, one of the bar staff heard a loud whispered voice say "It's here, It's here." Thinking at first one of the other staff was having a game with her, she rushed into the bar, only to find that they were all busy serving. There was no way they could have been responsible and since that occasion others have heard similar whispering in the vicinity of the toilets.

On another occasion the caretaker, who lives in the flat over the pub, clearly heard the noise of barrels being moved in the locked cellar; going down stairs expecting to find burglars, he noticed that the noise was getting louder and sounded as if barrels were being dragged across the concrete floor.

He first noticed that the door, the only entrance to the cellar, was still locked so, as quietly as possible, he unlocked it and swung the door wide open. The noise stopped immediately. Switching on the lights, he was flabbergasted to find that everything was in order, not a thing out of place!!

Other strange things have happened in this cellar. Many times the gas taps have been turned off although nobody has been down there and on one occasion the supply of beer stopped through lack of pressure. One of the staff went down to check the barrel, but it was still half full but the gas tap had been turned off, although it had been working perfectly prior to the stoppage. When the gas was turned on all went well for about half an hour then the flow stopped again - the tap was again turned off although nobody had been down the cellar since the first stoppage!

At times, at a point half way up the stairs that lead to the first floor functions room, there is a strong smell of a cheap perfume. This usually happens about 4 o'clock in the morning.

Whether any of these phenomenon can be put down to past smuggling activity is open to speculation but, as with the playful poltergeist, one thing is for certain - they are quite harmless.

WEELEY

THE MYSTERY OF THE POND

There is an old story that many years ago, a carriage drawn by two horses, left The Lodge, one evening after a party. When it was almost level with Weeley church, the horses suddenly veered off the track straight into a large pond which at that time was said to have been very deep, deep enough to completely swallow up both the horses and the carriage; whether the passengers survived or not is not recorded, but certainly the horses and carriage were never seen again.

Parishioners leaving the church late at night have often heard the sounds of iron clad wheels approaching along the lane, followed by a splashing in the pond.

The pond is still there today, but now so silted up that it is only a couple of feet deep. Thus leaving one wondering, if ever the pond should be cleaned out to its original depth, just what would be revealed!

GREAT BROMLEY

STRANGE HAPPENINGS AT SEVEN RIVERS

Seven Rivers Cheshire Home, Gt Bromley, is a nursing home specializing in the care, general well-being and rehabilitation of people with physical and/or mental disability.

Some of the patients are so incapacitated that they are unable to move their limbs at all and have to rely entirely on the nurses for their every need.

One such patient managed to relate a strange occurence he experienced early in 1993.

Being completely disabled, he was only able to move his jaw and by a rocking movement just move his head a fraction of an inch.

One night he was put to bed as usual, lying on his back with an alarm placed near his head so that in an emergency, he could rock his head and make contact to set off the alarm which was plugged into a socket on the wall.

Some time during the night, he was aware of some unseen force gently lifting him up and over the side of his bed, which had automatically been raised by the nurse before leaving him, and he was then very gently laid on the floor and covered with a blanket.

The whole sequence of events was carried out so gently that the facial alarm was not disturbed and the lead was not disconnected from the wall.

When the nurses came the next morning, they were horrified to find their patient soundly asleep on the floor.

The mystery still remains - how was it possible for him to be lifted so gently so as not to activate the alarm, when normally it took three trained nurses to lift him; also why should any force do such a thing? Was it some form of psychic healing?

Perhaps the answer will never be revealed. As far as can be ascertained there is no history of psychic activity having taken place there before.

COLCHESTER

THE COLCHESTER CASTLE MYSTERY

In the late 1930's, a man is said to have agreed to spend the night locked inside the Colchester Castle for a £200 bet.

Arrangements were made with the authorities and certain conditions agreed, such as there should be no liability whatsoever on the authorities and the person involved should enter the Castle at eight o'clock in the evening, and be let out at eight o'clock the next morning. The keys to be held by the officer in charge of the castle at the time.

At eight o'clock on the appointed day, the keys were duly turned on him. A small crowd turned up to witness the event, but they soon dispersed after the official held up the keys for all to see.

About ten o'clock, people passing by in the High Street saw a figure running about on the roof of the castle waving his arms and shouting.

At first nobody took much notice, thinking it was a practical joke, until at last, one man did take the matter seriously and sent for the fire brigade.

When the fire appliance arrived, complete with a large turntable ladder, the ladder was just long enough to reach the roof to enable the firemen to climb up to the unfortunate man.

It was not until then did they realise that the man they had come to rescue had become a gibbering raving lunatic.

After nearly an hours' struggle, they eventually managed to get him down to the ground where a doctor sedated him and took him off to Severalls Hospital.

By all accounts he never regained his sanity and died a few months later.

Just what had scared him so much was never discovered and the whole incident was hushed up.

With the outbreak of war eminent, everyone had more important things to worry about, but for the people involved with the bet, the whole situation must have weighed heavily on their conscience.

COLCHESTER

THE MYSTERY OF WARD 8

A strange tale was related by a now retired nurse who was often in charge of Ward 8, in Colchester's Essex County Hospital.

Ward 8 was closed for a time to be modernised and redecorated. When it re-opened, it was used to accommodate patients suffering from cancer and who were being treated by chemotherapy.

This treatment usually caused the patient to loose their hair, so patients are often given wigs to wear to help them to feel more comfortable.

One such patient was a little old lady who was so weak that she was seldom able to leave her bed, even then she had to be helped.

The nurse was on duty one night, sitting at her table in the ward checking over her reports, the lights were subdued, yet bright enough to have a clear view of the ward.

Everything was quiet and normal, but never-the-less, something made her look up from her papers, and to her amazement she saw the little old lady dressed all in white, walking down the ward, stopping at each bed in turn and facing the occupant, holding her hands together, with her lips moving as if in prayer.

She went up one side of the ward and down the other until she came to the last bed. At this point the nurse stood up and was about to approach her, when something whizzed past her head with a whoosh and suddenly there was no sign of the little old lady.

Going over to the patient's bed, the nurse was even more astonished to find her in bed fast asleep!!

The next morning as the nurse was about to go off duty, her attention was drawn to something lying on the floor just past her table. Stooping to pick it up, she recognised 'the thing' as being the little lady's wig!

We hope that you have enjoyed reading
'THE GHOSTS OF BORLEY' and the other stories.

Have you also read its companion books by the same author:

'HAUNTED CLACTON'

'THE HAUNTED COLCHESTER AREA'

'THE TERRIBLE TREASURE HOLT STORY'

All these books are now available from most book shops and newsagents or signed copies can be obtained direct from:
Wesley's Publications, 61 Lymington Avenue,
Clacton-on-Sea, CO15 4QE
Price £3.95 each. Post free.

The publishers would welcome any stories or experiences of Ghosts and Hauntings in Essex or Suffolk for future books.